"It's simple en[ough]... [I'm] a wizard and [I was turned into] a boy by a wit[ch]... [What's the matter] with you?"

"What's the matter with *me*?" said Joe.

Just then a teacher rang the bell right next to Joe, and he nearly jumped out of his skin again. But at least he could get away from Billy. He almost ran into the classroom. This is great, he thought. The only person who wants to talk to me is completely crazy.

It was going to be a long day.

Young Corgi books are perfect when you are looking for great books to read on your own. They are full of exciting stories and entertaining pictures. There are funny books, scary books, spine-tingling stories and mysterious ones. Whatever your interests you'll find something in Young Corgi to suit you: from families to football, from animals to ghosts. The books are written by some of the most famous and popular of today's children's authors, and by some of the best new talents, too.

Whether you read one chapter a night, or devour the whole book in one sitting, you'll love Young Corgi Books. The more you read, the more you'll want to read!

Other Young Corgi Books to get your teeth into:
THE PROMPTER by Chris d'Lacey
NITERACY HOUR by John Dougherty
THE CAT LADY by Dick King-Smith
DIARY DAYS by Gillian Potts
JOE v. THE FAIRIES by Emily Smith

BILLY WIZARD

written and illustrated by

Chris Priestley

For my son, Adam

BILLY WIZARD
A YOUNG CORGI BOOK : 0 552 54689 5

Published in Great Britain by Young Corgi,
an imprint of Random House Children's Books

This edition published 2005

1 3 5 7 9 10 8 6 4 2

Text and illustrations copyright © Chris Priestley, 2005
Illustration on page 37 by Adam Priestley

The right of Chris Priestley to be identified as the author of this work has been
asserted in accordance with the Copyright, Designs and Patents Act 1988

Papers used by Random House Children's Books are natural, recyclable
products made from wood grown in sustainable forests. The manufacturing
processes conform to the environmental regulations of the country of origin.

Set in 15/20pt Bembo Schoolbook

Young Corgi Books are published by Random House Children's Books,
61–63 Uxbridge Road, London W5 5SA,
a division of The Random House Group Ltd,
in Australia by Random House Australia (Pty) Ltd,
20 Alfred Street, Milsons Point, Sydney, NSW 2061, Australia,
in New Zealand by Random House New Zealand Ltd,
18 Poland Road, Glenfield, Auckland 10, New Zealand
and in South Africa by Random House (Pty) Ltd, Isle of Houghton,
Corner Boundary Road & Carse O'Gowrie, Houghton 2198, South Africa

THE RANDOM HOUSE GROUP Limited Reg. No. 954009
www.**kids**at**random**house.co.uk

A CIP catalogue record for this book is available from the British Library.

Printed and bound in Great Britain by
Cox & Wyman Ltd, Reading, Berkshire

Contents

Chapter 1

New Boys

"You'll be fine, sweetheart," said Joe's mother as they reached the gates of his new school. The playground was full of chattering children and their chattering parents.

"I know," said Joe grumpily. He wished his mum would stop making a fuss.

But even so, he did start to feel just

a little bit nervous. After all, when he
and his mum and dad had looked
round the school, the children had
been in assembly. It had almost been
like looking round an empty school.

Now the children were all grouped
in huddles, talking and laughing.

Every now and then one of them would look across at Joe and then turn back to his or her friends and talk and laugh some more.

Joe looked up at his mother and she did her best to smile. She didn't know anyone either and the other parents were looking at her just like the children were looking at him. She leaned down and gave him a kiss on the cheek.

"I hope Dad's getting on all right," she said. "It's his first day too."

Joe didn't say anything. He was cross with his dad. All this was his dad's fault. His dad's new job was the whole reason why they had moved to Little Hartley in the first place.

. Once upon time the word "new" had seemed like a good word – new book, new bike, new car. Not now.

Now *everything* was new: new house, new job, new school and *no* friends. If Joe could have waved a magic wand, he would have turned everything back to how it was when they lived in Gaston. Everything had been fine then.

At that moment, one of the children waved at him, smiled and shouted, "Hi!" and Joe smiled and waved and was about to shout, "Hi!" back when he realized the boy wasn't waving to him at all but to someone behind him, and Joe pretended to scratch his head instead of wave and he could feel his ears going red. Then suddenly a teacher nearby rang a hand bell and Joe and his mum nearly jumped out of their skins.

"Well . . . bye bye, sweetheart," said his mother. "Have a lovely day."

"Bye, Mum," said Joe.

All the other children knew exactly what to do. They got into different queues and waited for their teachers to come out and lead them into the classrooms. The teacher they had met when they looked round the school –

Miss Parker — smiled at Joe and waved him over and he nervously joined the end of the queue.

He looked round at his mother and remembered that she was starting a new job too. He wanted to shout, "Good luck!" but thought he had

better not. She blew him a kiss and Joe followed the children through the doors into his new classroom.

Inside, all the other children bustled about, hanging their coats on their pegs and putting their book bags in one plastic basket and their playtime snacks in another. Joe just stood there

looking lost until the
classroom assistant,
Mrs Michaels, came
over and helped him.

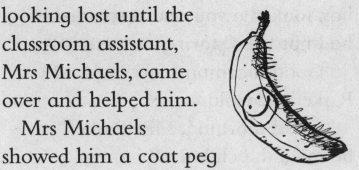

Mrs Michaels
showed him a coat peg
he could use and he put his
book bag with the others. Mum had
given him a banana for his snack
and had drawn a smiley face on the
skin. Joe smiled but put it in the
basket smiley face down, just in case
the other children thought it was silly.
You couldn't be too careful.

Mrs Michaels showed him through
into the classroom and Joe sat down
on the carpet in front of Miss Parker
as she looked through some papers
on her lap and got ready to read the
register. A boy nearby stared at Joe
until Joe looked back, and then the

boy looked away and pretended he had not been staring at Joe at all.

"Good morning, class," said Miss Parker suddenly.

"Good morning, Miss Parker!" boomed the children.

Joe tried to join in but was a little behind the others so that when everyone else had gone quiet, there was just Joe mumbling ". . . Miss Parker" all on his own. There were giggles and Joe tried to stop his ears going red again.

"Now then, class," said Miss Parker, clapping her hands together, "I wonder if any of you can remember what it was like when you first started school?" A boy nearby put his hand up. "Yes, Thomas?" she asked.

"Miss, miss, I saw a fire engine on the way to school today, miss. I reckon there must have been a fire somewhere 'cos it had its lights on and everything," he said excitedly.

"Did it, Thomas?" she said with a smile. "Well, I'm sure that was very exciting, but can anyone remember their first day at school?"

The boy who had been staring at Joe put his hand up.

"Neil," said Miss Parker. "What can you remember?"

"It was scary, miss," he said. "And I didn't know anybody." A couple of the girls giggled and the boy called Neil went a little red in the face.

"That's enough,

9

Molly," said Miss Parker, frowning at the most giggly of the girls. "It was scary. Yes, Neil. Starting school can be very scary, can't it? And not knowing anybody can be a bit frightening too." Everyone nodded.

"Well, then," she went on, "I want you all to close your eyes and have a little think about what it might be like if today was your first day at school and you didn't know anyone."

Everyone closed their eyes. Joe wasn't sure if he was meant to close *his* eyes. This *was* his first day, so he didn't have to imagine it. A boy with curly hair picked his nose.

"OK," said Miss Parker. "Now I want you all to hold onto that thought of what it feels like to start a new school, because as you may already have noticed we have two

new children in the class today . . ."

Two? thought Joe, and he looked around trying to guess who the other new boy or girl was.

"So let's give our new classmates a big welcome," said Miss Parker, "and make them feel at home. Joe" – she

beckoned him towards her – "and you, Billy. Up you come and let everyone see you. Come on now. No one's going to eat you."

Joe felt his ears going red again as he got to his feet and walked over to stand next to Miss Parker. The boy called Billy had been sitting right at the back and took a little longer to get there. He was about Joe's height, but skinnier with a mop of blond hair. He looked miserable.

The morning passed quicker than Joe had expected and all of a sudden it was playtime. Not knowing anyone in his class did not seem to matter when they were listening to a story or drawing a picture, but now, as he looked out on a playground full of children, Joe's heart sank once more.

He scanned the playground. He

had to find the cool kids. The last thing he wanted was to accidentally end up making friends with the losers. These first few minutes might decide who he was going to play with for the next few years.

The children were all rushing about in groups, intent on whatever game they were playing. Joe just stood by the wall and watched. Eventually one of the boys from his class – the one called Neil – came over.

"Do you want to play?" he asked.

"Don't know," said Joe suspiciously. Neil was the one who had said he had been scared on his first day. Joe remembered how the girls had giggled. You had to be so careful. "What are you playing?"

"Dog, Cat, Monkey," he said.

"Cat, Mouse, what?" said Joe, frowning.

"Didn't they play Dog, Cat, Monkey at your old school?"

"No, they did not!" exclaimed Joe.

"What *did* they play then?" asked Neil.

"Loads of stuff," said Joe. "Loads of *really* cool stuff."

"Like what?"

"Like . . . like . . . er . . . like . . ." began Joe, but the truth of it was that he could not remember a single game from his old school. Neil smiled and walked off. Joe muttered to himself and was still muttering when he realized there was someone standing next to him. It was Billy – the other new boy.

"Hi," said Billy.

"Hi," said Joe.

"What a dump," said Billy.

"Yeah," said Joe. "They tried to get you to play Dog, Mouse, Turkey yet?"

"You mean Dog, Cat, Monkey?" said Billy. "No. I love that game, don't you?" Joe muttered something

16

under his breath. "Games like that almost make me forget about the spell and who I really am. For a while, anyway."

"The *spell*?" asked Joe. "Who you *really* are?"

Billy glanced nervously about and stepped a little closer. Joe stepped a little back.

"Look," said Billy. "I shouldn't tell you this. It's against the rules, if you know what I mean."

"Not really, no."

"It's just that I'm not really a boy," said Billy.

"You're a girl?" asked Joe.

"No, you idiot," said Billy. "I'm a man. A grown-up."

Joe squinted at him suspiciously. "Well, you certainly *look* like a boy."

"Well of course!" said Billy. "What

kind of spell would it be if I didn't?
Agatha may be an crazy old witch,
but she knows her stuff."

"A witch?" Joe started to back off
again.

"Haven't you been listening?" said

Billy with a sigh. "She caught me off
guard. You'd think an old wizard like me
would know better, but there you are."

"A wizard?" said Joe.

"Will you stop repeating everything I say?" said Billy. "It's simple enough. I'm a wizard and I've been turned into a boy by a witch. What's the matter with you?"

"What's the matter with *me*?" said Joe.

Just then a teacher rang the bell right next to Joe, and he nearly jumped out of his skin again. But at least he could get away from Billy. He almost ran into the classroom. This is great, he thought. The only person who wants to talk to me is completely crazy.

It was going to be a long day.

Chapter 2

Weirdo

"So," said Joe's mother when she
picked him up from school. "How
was your first day?"

"OK," he muttered.

"Did you make any friends?" she
asked.

"Not really," he said. "Did you?"

His mother laughed. "No, not
really," she said. "We'll both have to
do better tomorrow."

Joe tried to smile, but it was like his
face had forgotten how.

"It's nice to be able to walk home

from school, isn't it?" said his mum.

"I suppose so," said Joe. "But what if it rains?"

"Then we'll bring an umbrella, silly."

Joe shrugged.

When they got home, Joe watched TV for a while, but there was nothing on that he liked. He went to his bedroom and lay on his bed and flicked through a book his gran had sent him through the post. A few pages in he came across a full-page illustration showing a wizard in long robes and a purple pointy hat all covered with stars and moons.

He had a wand and there were sparks of magic streaming out of it. Joe thought of Billy at school and smiled.

"Crazy," he said to himself.

It would be cool to be a wizard though. If something was not how you liked it, you could just change it – *shazam!* You would never have to put up with anything you didn't like ever again. He could magic himself up a couple of really cool friends. It would be great.

Joe's father came home from work later. Joe listened to him go on and on about his new job and how great it was and how it was the best thing he had ever done. The people in his office were great and the job was really interesting and he was getting paid more money too. He asked Joe how *his* first day had been.

"I don't know," muttered Joe.

"Well, what did you do?"

"Can't remember," said Joe.

"Not even one teeny-weeny thing?" asked his dad with a smile.

"No," said Joe sternly.

"Come on, Joe," said his dad. "Don't be like that."

But Joe *was* like that for the rest of the evening. He was like that through dinner and right through to bedtime. He hardly spoke a word until he said "Good night" to his mum after she had read a chapter from the book his gran had sent.

"Try to cheer up, sweetheart," she said. "And try not to give Dad such a hard time. It's not easy for him either, you know."

"Hmmph!" said Joe. "He's having a

great time. You heard him."

Joe's mum smiled. "He doesn't want us to worry. But I've known Dad a lot longer than you, you know. He had a difficult day today. I can tell. He's very shy, your dad."

"Shy?" said Joe. "Dad?"

"Yes. Shy," said his mum. "As a mouse. You never see him when he has to talk to people he doesn't know. He gets so nervous. You wouldn't

recognize him. Now off to sleep and
let's see if you can't wake up in a
better mood."

"OK," said Joe. "I'll try."

But all Joe could think of was all
the things they had left behind in
Gaston and how different everything
was here and how he hated it. Joe
and his dad sometimes used to get a
video out of the video shop and buy
fish and chips. They would never find
fish and chips like those. They were
the best fish and chips in the whole
world.

Joe snuggled into Fred Bear, his
teddy, and tried to think nice
thoughts about school the next day.
Laura Patterson, who lived a few
doors down from him in Gaston, said
he was too old to have a teddy, but
his mum said you were never too old

to have a teddy and anyway, what did Laura Patterson know about anything?

Joe liked to talk to Fred before he went to sleep and it made him feel better to have someone to tell his troubles to. He seemed to talk to Fred more than ever these days. In fact, just to be on the safe side, he decided to go and get Floppy Pig, Monster, Furry Tiger and Dog as well.

Joe piled them up along the pillow, leaving a gap for his head, and snuggled down again with Floppy Pig flopping over his ear. Furry Tiger tickled his nose as he tried to think of good things, but the only thing he could think of that made him smile was Billy.

"Crazy," whispered Joe to himself and fell asleep.

The following day Joe's dad was
leaving for work just as Joe came
downstairs for his breakfast.

"Good luck at school today," said
his father, ruffling his hair.

"Yeah," mumbled Joe.

"Bye," shouted his father in the
direction of the kitchen.

"Bye," his mother shouted back.
"Have a good day."

"Thanks." Joe's dad opened the
front door and walked over to his car.
Joe watched quietly as he drove
away.

Joe ate his breakfast and got

washed and dressed and brushed his teeth, and then he and his mother walked down the road to school. When they walked into the playground, Neil from his class smiled and said, "Hi."

"Oh, hi," said Joe.

Then Billy walked up to him, looking around suspiciously as usual. "Joe, Joe," he said, "I've got to talk to you. Speak to you later, yeah?"

"Yeah, sure," said Joe.

Billy's mother called Billy over and was smoothing down his hair. Joe smiled. Some wizard, he thought.

"I thought you said you hadn't spoken to anyone," said Joe's mother.

"Well, I hadn't really," said Joe. "Just . . . just . . . Neil . . . and that boy over there – Billy. He's a bit weird. He thinks he's a wizard."

"A wizard?" She smiled. "I'm sure he's just having a game with you. Anyway, I knew you'd make friends."

Mrs Michaels rang the bell and Joe and his mum jumped in fright.

"I do wish they wouldn't do that," said his mother. "Have a lovely day."

"Yeah," said Joe.

"Love you," said his mother, giving him a kiss. The girl from his class called Molly saw them and giggled.

"Yeah." Joe could feel his ears going red again.

He trooped into class with the rest of the children. It was not so bad this time, because he now knew where to put his book bag and his snack. He hung his coat up on the peg that now said JOE, opposite one

that was now labelled BILLY.

The morning went reasonably well. They had the end of a story about a flying horse and then they had to write one of their own and do a picture to go with it. Joe liked writing

Joe

and he was good at drawing, so he began to relax a little and almost enjoy himself.

But at playtime he stood in his place by the wall, wishing he had not been so snooty about Neil's offer of playing Dog, Cat, Monkey. It looked fun. He sighed and gazed down at his shoes. Maybe it was not too late to change his mind. He could always ask to join in.

When he looked up again, a football was flying straight towards his face. In blind panic and without even thinking, he put his hands up to meet it and caught the football in mid air, a couple of centimetres from

his nose. When he lowered the ball, Billy was standing right next to him.

"Good catch," he said.

"Er . . . yeah. I suppose," said Joe, staring at him. Someone whistled and he could see a group of children waving at him to throw them the ball. He tossed it back. He hated football. "What did you want to talk to me about?"

Billy looked baffled.

"This morning," hinted Joe. "You said you needed to talk to me."

"Did I?"

"Yes," said Joe with a sigh.

"Can't remember," said Billy.

Joe frowned. "I saw your mum this morning."

Billy looked a little embarrassed. "She's not my mum," he said.

"Sorry," said Joe. "I just thought—"

"That's Agatha," whispered Billy with a snarl.

"The, er, *witch* that turned you into

a boy?" asked Joe, raising an eyebrow. "Hmmm. She didn't look much like a witch."

"Of course she didn't. You don't think she's going to come to school all green and warty, do you? Then everyone would know, wouldn't they?"

"I suppose they would," said Joe. "But she tidied your hair and everything."

"Oh she's good. She's very good."

"Look," said Joe, getting cross. "You are not a wizard, OK? You are not a wizard and your mother's not a witch!"

"What are you two going on about?" said a voice behind them.

They turned, and standing next to Joe was a stocky boy from a couple of years above them, whom Joe had

already noticed. He always seemed to have a group of boys with him. His name was Rick. He had short ginger hair and freckles all over his face – even on his ears.

"Look, some of us are playing football on the sports field this Saturday. Saw that amazing catch you made just then. We need a goalie. Fancy a game?"

If there was one thing Joe hated more than playing football, it was being in goal when he was playing football.

"Yeah," he said. "That'd be great."

"Cool," said Rick.

"I *am* a wizard!" said Billy.

"What did he say?" asked Rick.

"He says he's a wizard," said Joe.

"Weirdo." Rick turned back to Joe. "Saturday – about ten o'clock," he said as he walked away.

"Cool," said Joe.

"*Cool*," repeated Billy in a smarmy voice.

"*I am a wizard!*" repeated Joe in a silly voice.

"I am!" shouted Billy. "If I wasn't a wizard," he went on, raising his hands above his head, holding his hands like claws and staring after Rick, "would I be able to do *this*?"

 Billy threw out his arms in the direction of Rick's retreating figure and waggled his fingers about while looking

boggle-eyed. Nothing happened.

"Wow," said Joe in a bored voice.

Billy hunched his shoulders, screwed his hands into fists and stomped off towards the quiet area of the playground, where he sat on a bench and muttered to himself.

"What a weirdo," said Joe. "What a total weirdo."

Chapter 3

Wizards Like Chocolate Cake

At the end of the day Joe joined all the other children to fetch his coat to go home. Billy was collecting his coat from his peg on the other side of the narrow cloakroom. Molly Mason and her friend Charlotte were chattering away as usual.

"Don't forget I'm bringing Little Danny in tomorrow," said Molly.

"He's so cute," said Charlotte as they both went back into the classroom to line up.

"Who's little Danny?" asked Joe.

"Don't know," said Billy. "Her baby brother, I think."

Neil squeezed along towards them. "I saw you talking to Rick Bellows," he said above the din.

"So?" said Joe.

"He's trouble. You should stay away from him."

"Should I?" said Joe crossly. He was beginning to get annoyed with the way Neil kept interfering.

"Yes," said Neil. "You should."

"Well, he wants me to play football with him and I said I would," said Joe.

Neil tutted and walked off shaking his head. Joe scowled and followed him back to the classroom, where everyone quietened down and lined up in a queue ready to go home.

When Joe marched out into the

playground, he could see his mum talking to one of the other mothers. As he got closer he realized that it was Billy's mother. Joe grinned to himself. If Mum only knew, he thought to himself, that she was talking to the hideous Agatha, the Wicked Witch of Wherever–it–was.

As Joe walked up to them, his mother gave him a kiss and said to Billy's mother, "Here he is. This is Joe."

"How are you, Joe?" said Billy's mother.

"Very well, thank you," said Joe. "How are you?"

"I'm very well, thank you," she said with a very un–witchy smile. "What a polite young man. And here's Billy."

Billy shuffled up with his hands in his pockets and his shirt hanging out

of his trousers on one side. He
scowled at each of them in turn.
Joe's mother backed off slightly.

"Now then, Billy," said Billy's
mother. "Joe's mother here has very
kindly said you can go back with
them to Joe's house and play for a
while. What do you say?"

Billy mumbled something that could have been "Thank you" but could have been many things.

Joe's mother looked as though she was already regretting making the offer and when she looked at Joe, she saw him frowning darkly at Billy.

"That's settled then," said Billy's mother. "I'll pick you up at five thirty. Behave yourself, Billy," she added as she turned to go home, a worried look flickering across her face.

They started to walk home, both boys scowling. Joe saw Rick Bellows getting into his father's car, a smooth silvery sports car. Joe had admired it the day before.

"Rick!" he called with a wave. "See you tomorrow!"

Rick looked baffled for a minute,

as though he had never seen Joe
before in his life. "What?" he
snapped, but then he remembered.
"Oh, yeah, right." Then he spotted
Billy and patted his father on the
arm. "Hey, Dad, there's that weird kid
I told you about!" He chuckled
loudly. "Look at him. What a dork!"
Rick's father joined in the chuckling
as they got into the car. They put on
matching sunglasses, the engine
roared and they drove noisily away.

"What a horrid boy," said Joe's mum.

"Who, Rick?" said Joe. "Nah, he's all right." Billy snorted. "At least he doesn't think he's a wizard!" hissed Joe.

"What's all this about wizards?" asked Joe's mother.

Neither boy answered. They plodded silently along after her, scowling all the way to Joe's house.

"I've got some chocolate cake, Billy," said Joe's mother as she unlocked the front door. "Would you like some?"

"Yes please," said Billy.

"Take your shoes off, boys, and sit yourselves down," she told them. "I'll bring it through in a minute." And she went off into the kitchen.

They took off their shoes and Billy

followed Joe into the dining room.
Joe's mother came through with the
cake and some apple juice.

"So wizards eat chocolate cake
then," said Joe as soon as she had left
the room.

"Yeah," said Billy, picking
up a huge slice of cake.
"Some do. A few do. I
do." He took a huge
bite, smearing his nose
with chocolate cream.

Joe was trying to stay
annoyed with Billy but
he couldn't stop himself
from laughing, and Billy joined him,
almost choking on his cake.

"That's better," said Joe's mum,
putting her head round the door.
"I thought you two would never
cheer up. Why don't you go up to

your room, Joe, and show Billy all your toys? I don't mind how much mess you make as long as you clear it up later."

So Joe dragged box after box out of his cupboards and down from his shelves and the two boys played happily for the rest of the afternoon, setting up a huge game involving all Joe's animals, his knights and his battery-powered spaceship.

Joe's dad popped in to see him when he came back from work. "Hi, Joe – er, children," he said, stopping cautiously in the doorway when he saw Billy.

"Hi, Dad," said Joe, without looking up. "This is Billy. From school."

"Oh . . . er . . . hi, Billy," said Joe's dad a little nervously.

"Hello," said Billy as the spaceship

zoomed out of control towards a group of knights.

Joe's father stood there for a few moments looking lost, twiddling his fingers, then left them to it. Not long after, they heard the doorbell and Billy's mother was calling him to go home.

"He wasn't any trouble, I hope," she said as Billy put his shoes back on.

"None at all," said Joe's mother. "I barely knew they were there. They got on like magic."

Joe and his mother waved from the front door as Billy and his mother drove away. Billy wasn't so bad after all, thought Joe, even if he was a bit crazy. Perhaps he had been too hard on him.

"Billy is sweet, isn't he?" said his mother, closing the door.

Joe shuddered. Sweet? *Sweet?* Urggggh! It was one thing for Billy to be bonkers, but *sweet* — that was too much. This is what happened if you were not careful about choosing your friends and let your mother get involved. *Sweet!*

Chapter 4

Vanishing Rick

Joe was in a much better mood when he went to school the next day. He chatted to his mum on the way and they laughed and joked just like they used to when they lived in Gaston.

"I'm glad you've made a friend like Billy," said his mother as they walked past the war memorial. "He's so much nicer than those awful boys you got in with when we lived in Gaston."

"Who?" asked Joe defensively.

"Carl Denton and his gang," said his mother.

Joe frowned. "Carl was all right."

"Carl was not all right," said his mother. "Carl was a menace. He was always getting in trouble. He was a nasty bully and you followed him round like a little puppy."

"No I didn't," said Joe.

"Never mind." His mum sighed. "It doesn't matter now. Carl is in Gaston and we're here. Hopefully there aren't any boys like him at your new school anyway."

"Mum," said Joe as they arrived at the school gates, "would it be OK if I played football on the sports field on

Saturday morning?"

"I suppose so," she said. "Who with?"

Joe remembered his mum saying what a horrid boy Rick was. "Oh, you know, with, er, Billy and, er, this other boy – Neil."

"Yes, why not," said his mum.

"Great!"

"I can do my shopping in the afternoon instead, I suppose. And it will give me a chance to chat to Billy's mum. She seems very nice."

"But . . . but . . ." began Joe.

"You didn't think I was going to let you go wandering round the village on your own, did you?"

"But Mum," said Joe.

"Never mind 'but Mum'," she said. "I promise I won't laugh if you fall over."

Great, thought Joe as he said good-
bye and tramped into the classroom.
He had finally got in with the really
cool kids in the school and now his
mum was going to turn up with him
like he was a baby or something.
There must be something he could
do. It was so unfair.

As Joe was leaving the
classroom at play time, he saw that
Molly Mason was talking to
Miss Parker and crying.
Then he heard her
say, "He's disappeared,
miss. I can't find him
anywhere."

As Joe walked out into
the playground Rick came over.

"Still on for Saturday?" he asked.

"Yeah, sure," said Joe. "Definitely."

Billy walked past and Rick pointed

his thumb at him. "Not bringing that weirdo with you, I hope," he said.

"Nah," said Joe. "Course not."

"Good," said Rick. "See you later."

Joe had not realized but Neil had been standing nearby and wandered over, scowling at him.

"What's the matter with you?" asked Joe.

"I thought Billy was your friend," he said.

"Yeah . . . no . . . not really," stammered Joe.

"You always seem to be talking to him," said Neil. "I thought he went round your house last night."

"Well, yeah – he did. So what?"

Neil muttered something under his breath.

"What?" said Joe.

"Look, what do you want to hang

around with someone like that for anyway?" asked Neil.

"You mean Billy?" said Joe.

"No," said Neil. "I mean Rick."

"It's only a game of football. That's all. What's it got to do with you anyway?"

"Nothing," said Neil.

"Nothing," said Joe. "That's right. Exactly. Nothing. OK."

Neil wandered off and Joe scowled after him.

"What's up with you?" asked Billy, who had suddenly appeared at his side.

"Nothing," said Joe. "That Neil is a bit of a whinger, isn't he?"

"Neil? Don't know. He seems all right. Not like some of the creeps in this place."

"Hah," said a voice behind them.

"If anyone's a creep in this school it's you, weirdo." It was Rick. He barged Billy out of the way and stood in front of Joe. "Got any money?"

"Money?" asked Joe.

"I'll pay you back on Saturday," Rick said, holding out his hand.

"No, sorry," said Joe. "I haven't got any."

Rick frowned.

Over Rick's shoulder Joe could see Billy raising his hands like he had before and flicking out his fingers towards Rick's back. Rick could tell by Joe's expression that something was happening behind him and turned round to find Billy there, frowning at him, arms outstretched.

"What are doing?" he asked.

"Yeah," said Joe. "What are you doing, Billy?"

Billy frowned even more but said nothing. Rick laughed and Joe laughed with him.

"Weirdo!" said Rick, and he grabbed Billy by the collar and almost pulled him off his feet. Then he shoved him as hard as he could and it was all Billy could do to stop himself falling over. Rick's friends started a chant of "Weirdo! Weirdo!"

Joe stopped laughing.

"Trying to make me look stupid, are you, weirdo?" said Rick, giving Billy another push. This time Billy *did* fall over.

"Hey," said Joe, shoving Rick in the back. "Leave him alone!"

Rick stopped and turned round. "What?" he said. The whole playground seemed to go silent.

"Leave him alone," said Joe, a little more quietly.

Rick started to walk back towards Joe with his fists clenched, when someone stepped between them.

"And what is going on here?" It was Miss Parker.

"Nothing, miss," said Rick.

"Nothing, miss," said Joe.

"Nothing, miss," said Billy.

"Good," she said. "Billy and Joe,

you can help me set things up for art, and Rick, you can . . . you can go somewhere else."

"Yes, miss," he said and slowly walked away across the playground.

"Do you want to get thumped?" hissed Joe at Billy as they followed Miss Parker towards the classroom. "I mean, if you do, that's fine. You're doing great."

"No, I don't want to get thumped," said Billy.

"Do you want *me* to get thumped?" asked Joe.

"No," said Billy.

"You've spoiled everything!" said Joe. "I was going to play football on Saturday, and now look what you've done with your stupid wizard rubbish! Why do you have to be so . . . so . . . *different*?"

"What's wrong with being different?"

"Well, you might not want to have any friends but I do!"

"Course I want to have friends!" said Billy. "But not ones like Rick Bellows!" He scowled and turned back towards the playground. He raised his arms and flicked out his fingers towards Rick, who still had his back to them as he returned to his little gang.

"Will you stop doing that!" hissed Joe, as Billy caught up with him at the classroom door.

Suddenly there was a huge bang and Joe's heart felt like it had just tried to jump out of his chest. He looked back towards the playground, and there was a wisp of bluish smoke drifting across it where Rick had

been standing only a few seconds before. Rick . . . Rick had *completely disappeared.*

Then Joe noticed a tiny white mouse running across the playground and heading for the caretaker's shed. He stood staring, his eyes wide open and his mouth not far behind. He couldn't believe what he had just seen.

"What's up with you?" said a voice beside him. It was Neil.

"What? Me?" said Joe. "What's up? Er . . . nothing . . . Nothing's up."

Neil gave him a funny look.

"Joe!" called Miss Parker. "Come on, come on. We haven't got all day!"

As he walked in, Molly Mason came out, her eyes red from crying.

"What's up?" asked Joe.

"It's Little Danny," she said, beginning to sob again. "He's vanished."

Chapter 5

Zapped!

Joe couldn't really concentrate on his work for the rest of the morning. He kept looking over at Billy, who was drawing away with his tongue sticking out, as if nothing had happened; as if he were just some ordinary boy.

"What did you do to Rick?" whispered Joe when he found Billy in his usual place in the quiet area at lunch break.

Billy held up his hand and frowned, flicking out his fingers. "I zapped him," he said with a grin. "That'll teach him." He repeated the move with his hands and chuckled.

Joe looked horrified. "But you can't just go round zapping people."

"Can't I?" said Billy. "Why's that then?"

"I . . . I . . . I don't know. You just can't."

"Anyway," Billy explained, "I don't just zap anybody. I only zapped Rick because he's horrible

and if anyone needed zapping, he did."

"But what happens when you zap someone?" asked Joe.

"Lots of things," said Billy. "Anything."

"Like what?"

"I might make them disappear," he said matter-of-factly. "I might turn them into a frog or a pig or a—"

Joe's eyes widened as he remembered what had happened at play time. "Or a mouse!" he shouted.

"Yeah," said Billy, looking a little strangely at Joe. "Or a mouse."

"But . . . but . . ." stammered Joe. "You can't go round turning people into mice just because you don't like them."

"Why not?" said Billy in a bored voice.

"Why not?" repeated Joe. "Why not?"

"Yeah," said Billy. "Why not?"

"Because you can't. That's why not! And what about Molly Mason's baby brother? What had little Danny done to annoy you?"

"What are you on about?" asked Billy. "I've never even seen her stupid brother."

"Oh yeah? And I suppose he just vanished on his own!"

"Are you all right?" said Billy. "You seem a bit odd."

"*Me* a bit odd?" said Joe. "That's a good one! If there's anyone a bit odd round here, it's you!"

"Well, what are you doing talking to me then?" asked Billy. "Why don't you go somewhere else?"

"I think I will!" said Joe. "Weirdo!"

"Maybe I ought to change *you* into something!" Billy lifted up his hands and pointed his fingers at Joe.

"No!" shouted Joe. "Don't be stupid!" He dived out of the way, hurling himself onto the tarmac of the play-ground, with his hands over his head. When he looked up Billy was gone and Neil was standing over him.

"I suppose this must be one of those really cool games you used to play at your old school," said Neil with a chuckle, and walked off.

Joe got up and dusted himself down.

He did his best to avoid Billy for the rest of the day, but although he avoided talking to him and standing near him, he found it impossible to avoid looking at him.

Joe watched Billy's every move. He looked like all the other children, except that he seemed more miserable most of the time. But nobody would ever have suspected that he was anything other than an ordinary boy.

Joe couldn't wait for the end of the school day, but when he walked over to the waiting parents, he got a shock. His mother was chatting and laughing with Billy's so-called mother, who, Joe now realized, must really be some kind of terrible witch, just like Billy had said.

"Hello, Joe," said his mum. "How was your day?"

"Er . . . hi, Mum . . ." said Joe, looking sideways at Billy's "mother".

"Are you OK?" asked his mum.

Joe didn't answer. He was too busy trying to see if he could see any sign of the witch beneath the disguise.

"Joe?" said his mother. "Are you all right?"

"What? Me?" said Joe finally. "Yeah . . . I'm all right . . ."

"Well, I've got a little surprise for you," she said. "Billy's mother has said you can go back with Billy for a while." Joe stared open-mouthed. "I'll pick you up about five thirty."

"No!"

"Joe?" said his mother. "What's the matter?"

"No! I can't!" said Joe, backing away.

Joe's mother looked at Billy's mother. Billy's mother looked at Joe's mother. They both shrugged.

"I'm so sorry," said Joe's mother.

"Joe is behaving very oddly."

"Oh that's all right," said Billy's mother. "Billy behaves oddly all the time. I'm used to it."

Billy suddenly appeared.

"Why are you always the last to come out?" said his mother.

"Don't know," said Billy.

"Well," said Joe's mother. "Maybe another time. Thanks for the offer anyway."

"What was all that about?" she asked, when she and Joe had walked to the end of the street. "That was very rude. Have you and Billy had some sort of fight?"

"No," said Joe. "Not really. It's complicated."

"Try and explain it to me," said his mum. "I'm quite clever when I want to be." She smiled at him.

Joe opened his mouth to begin, but could not think what to say. "You'd never believe me," he said. "*I* wouldn't believe me," he said. "And I *am* me."

His mother raised one eyebrow. "I see," she said, shaking her head.

Joe could not settle when he got home. He couldn't even concentrate on his favourite TV programme, so he went up to his room and flopped down on the bed. He picked up the book his gran had given him. He looked at the picture of the wizard again: although the wizard had a long white beard, there was something about the eyes that really did look like Billy.

Chapter 6

New Friends

"Do you know what happened to Rick yesterday?" said Neil at break time the next morning.

"Well . . . yeah," said Joe, a little relieved to be able to share it with someone. "I didn't think anybody knew—"

"Everybody knows," said Neil. "Good riddance too."

"I know you didn't like him," said Joe, "but I'm not sure he deserved to be . . . you know . . ."

"He deserved a lot worse than

that, if you ask me."

"A lot worse?" said Joe, amazed at how calmly Neil was taking it.

"Doesn't strike me as so bad."

"Not so bad?" said Joe. "Are you kidding?"

"Look," said Neil. "He was horrible. He was a bully and he liked hurting people. He got off lightly."

"You call being turned into a

mouse getting off lightly?"

Neil stared at him. "Being turned into a what?"

"A mouse," said Joe.

Neil stared at him again. "Er . . . what are you talking about?"

"Rick," said Joe. "I'm talking about Rick."

"Rick has been taken out of our school by his mum and dad," said Neil. "They've been thinking of doing it for ages, but when he threw the firework yesterday and bunked off, that was the last straw."

"Firework?" said Joe in a daze. "Bunked off?"

"Are you all right?" asked Neil. "Rick's been sent to a private school by his parents. It's some tough place where they reckon he'll be knocked into shape. Serves him right."

"What's this about a firework?"
said Joe.

"What is the matter with you?"
said Neil. "You must be the only one
in the school who doesn't know. Rick
threw a banger at playtime. Didn't
you hear the bang? Then he climbed
over the fence and ran off."

"But what about the mouse?"
asked Joe.

"What mouse? Oh – you mean
Little Danny, Molly Mason's pet
mouse? She brought it into school to
show everyone and it escaped.
But what's that got to do with—?"

But Joe was gone.

Joe found Billy on his own in the quiet area of the playground.

"Hi," he said.

"Hi," said Billy without looking up from his feet.

"Sorry," said Joe. "You know, about yesterday and that."

"That's OK," said Billy.

"Rick's been sent to another school."

"Good," said Billy. He looked up at Joe. "Thanks for standing up to him for me."

"That's all right," said Joe, sitting down next to Billy. "I should have done it before, with you being my friend and that."

"Yeah?" said Billy.

"Definitely," said Joe.

"I'm not really a wizard, you know," said Billy.

"Yeah," said Joe. "I know."

"I wish I was."

"Yeah. Me too."

They sat in silence for a minute or two.

"It's not nice calling your mum a witch though, is it?" said Joe. "She seems really nice."

"She is," said Billy. "I don't know

why I do it." He sounded as though he was about to cry. "I don't mean to do it," he explained. "I got picked on by these older children at my last school and I started to make things up and pretend that I could get back at them. Once I pretended I was an alien from another planet who was in disguise and another time that I had super powers. I made all kinds of stuff up."

"Like being a wizard?" asked Joe.

Billy nodded. "Mum says I've got an over-active imagination. That's why she moved me to this school — because I told so many lies at my last one. Children called me names and I just got picked on even more. Now I've done the same thing here." He began to sob.

"Only to me and Rick," said Joe,

putting his arm round Billy's shoulder. "I don't mind and Rick's gone."

Billy smiled weakly. "What about Neil?"

"What about me?" asked Neil, wandering over at just that moment.

"Do you care that Billy's been saying he's a wizard?" said Joe.

"Not really," said Neil, sitting down next to them. "It is a bit crazy though."

"He's not going to do it any more," said Joe. "Are you, Billy?"

"No," said Billy, smiling.

"People picked on him at his last school," explained Joe.

"Well, the only person who was ever going to pick on you here was Rick and he's history," said Neil.

"Yeah," said Joe. "There was someone like him at my last school.

This boy called Carl."

"At least you stood up to him," said Neil. "No one ever stood up to Rick before. You'll be famous."

"I will?"

"He kicked that ball straight at you, on purpose," said Billy. "You know, when you caught it."

"Why didn't you say?" said Joe. "I hate football."

Billy and Neil laughed.

"You'd have hated it even more after a game with Rick," said Neil. "The last boy they persuaded to be in goal for them ended up with a black eye when he tried to stop Rick scoring."

Just then Joe noticed something out of the corner of his eye. A little white mouse had appeared between his feet, sniffing the air nervously. Billy and Neil followed his gaze downwards.

"Little Danny!" said all three of them together.

Joe bent down slowly and gently picked up the mouse in his cupped hands. "It looks frightened," he said.

"Well, so would you be if you were brought to a weird place where you didn't know anybody," said Neil.

"Yeah," said Joe. "I suppose so. Come on, let's take him back to Molly."

Molly Mason was overjoyed when Joe appeared with Little Danny. She was so happy, Joe was a bit worried that she was going to kiss him, but luckily she didn't.

"Where did you find him?" she asked.

"He found us really," said Joe. "He just kind of appeared like—"

"Like magic," said Billy.

Joe and Neil and Billy laughed.

"Listen," said Joe when they were getting their coats to go home. "Do you fancy playing football on Saturday morning?"

"I thought you hated football," said Billy.

"I do. I did. I mean, I might like it if I give it a go. It's just that I told my mum I was playing football with you both on Saturday, so we may as well."

"You mean you lied," said Billy with a grin.

"No . . . not exactly . . . well, yes —

kind of," said Joe, his ears going red.
"Well? What do you say?"

"Yeah," said Neil. "All right."

"OK," said Billy. "My mum won't
let me come on my own though. You
don't mind if she sits and watches, do

you? She won't be any trouble."

"Nah," said Neil. "Mine will want to come as well."

"Mine too," added Joe. "They can all talk to each other. They like that, mothers do."

"Yeah," said Neil.

"Great," said Joe. "That's settled then."

"And if you don't want to play football," said Neil, "me and Billy can teach you how to play Dog, Cat, Monkey."

"Cool," said Joe.

Joe's dad was at the school gate at the end of the day. He was standing on his own, well back from the rest of the parents. Joe could see that his father's ears were a bit red. He really *is* shy, he thought.

"Hi, Joe," he said. "Good day?"

"Yeah," said Joe. "It was all right.
How about yours?"

"Mine?" said his father. "It wasn't
bad, thanks."

"Really?" said Joe.

"Really."

"You're not just saying that?" asked
Joe.

"No." His dad smiled, his ears
turning a little redder. "I'm not just

saying that. What's brought this on?"

"Nothing," said Joe.

Billy wandered past them on his way to meet his mum. "See you," he said.

"Yeah," said Joe. "See you tomorrow."

"Hello there," said Joe's father. "It's Billy, isn't it? I was talking to your dad today. He works in the same building as me. Small world, eh?"

"He doesn't really work there, you know," said Billy, looking right and left and stepping a little closer. "He's undercover."

"Undercover?"

"Yeah, undercover," repeated Billy. "You know — in disguise. I'm not really supposed to say anything" — he dropped his voice to a whisper — "but he's really a policeman and he's there trying to catch a gang of jewel thieves. I can't say any more . . ." He looked right and left and then went off to meet his mum.

Joe shook his head. His dad looked baffled.

"Jewel thieves?" he said. "But we work for the council."

"Don't mind Billy. His mum says he's got an over-active imagination," said Joe.

"Oh," said his dad with a nod and a smile. "Listen, your mum's going to the cinema with a couple of people from work. How about we rent a DVD and grab some fish and chips?"

"Cool," said Joe.

So that is exactly what they did. They drove to the nearest fish and chip shop and sat on a low wall overlooking the sea to eat them. They both agreed that they were not quite the same as the fish and chips they used to get in Gaston.

They were better.

THE END